Manga boys Coloring Book

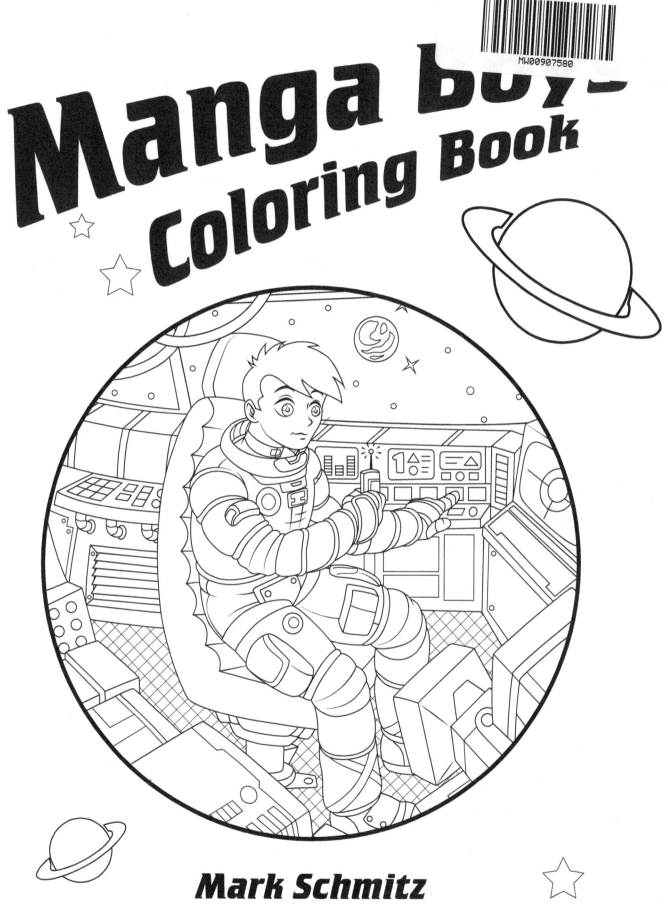

Mark Schmitz

Dover Publications, Inc.
Mineola, New York

NOTE

In this exciting coloring book you will encounter forty-six images depicting a variety of boys—all done in manga style! Manga is the famous Japanese style of cartooning, complete with wide-eyed figures, cuddly creatures, and an amazing array of situations. So get your pens, pencils, crayons, and colored markers ready to visit the land of manga where you will find boys playing sports, fighting robots, battling monsters, and much, much more!

Copyright

Copyright © 2013 by Dover Publications, Inc.
All rights reserved.

Bibliographical Note

Manga Boys Coloring Book is a new work, first published by Dover Publications, Inc., in 2013.

International Standard Book Number

ISBN-13: 978-0-486-49710-5
ISBN-10: 0-486-49710-0

Manufactured in the United States by Courier Corporation
49710001
www.doverpublications.com

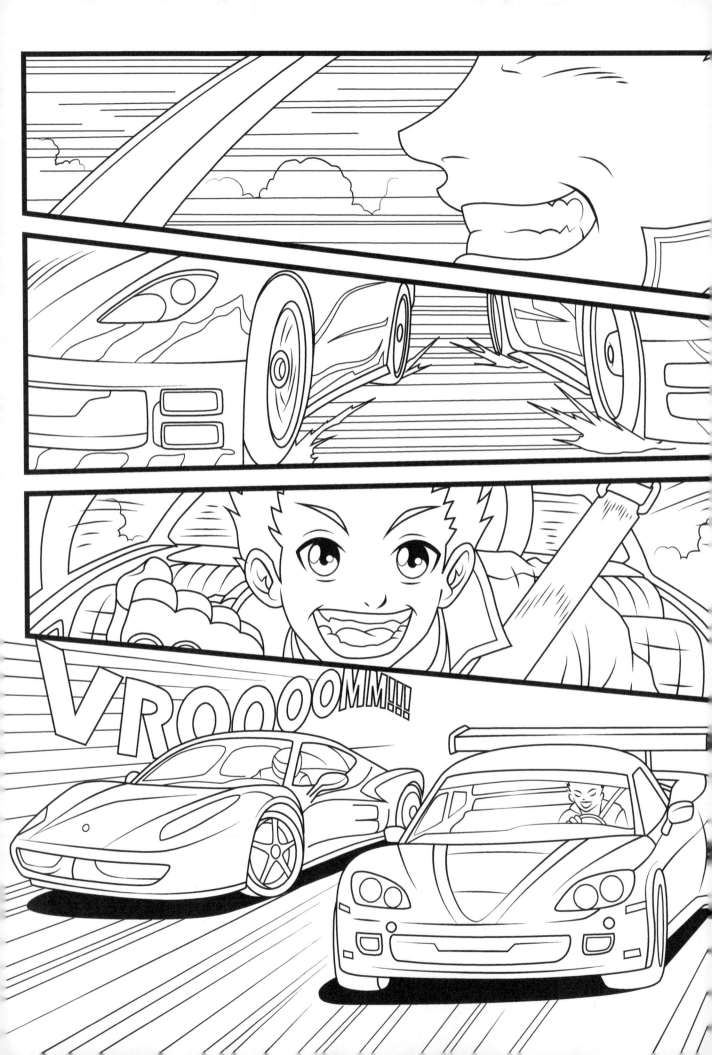

How to Draw... a Bat!

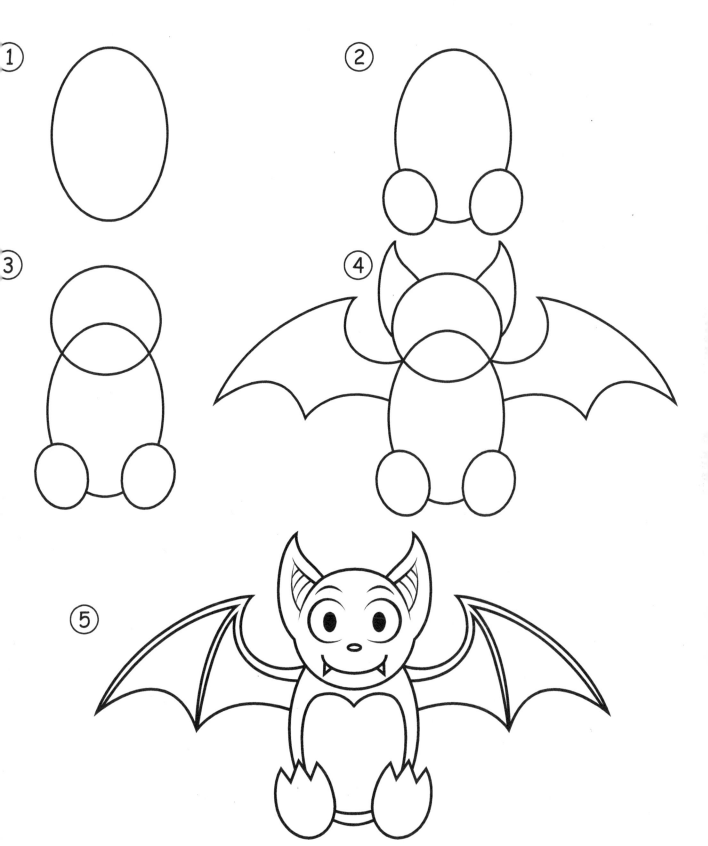

① ② ③ ④ ⑤

How to Draw... a Robot!

How to Draw... a Wolf!

How to Draw... a Ninja!